YEARLING BOOKS are designed especially to entertain and enlighten young people. Patricia Reilly Giff, consultant to this series, received her bachelor's degree from Marymount College and a master's degree in history from St. John's University. She holds a Professional Diploma in Reading and a Doctorate of Humane Letters from Hofstra University. She was a teacher and reading consultant for many years, and is the author of numerous books for young readers.

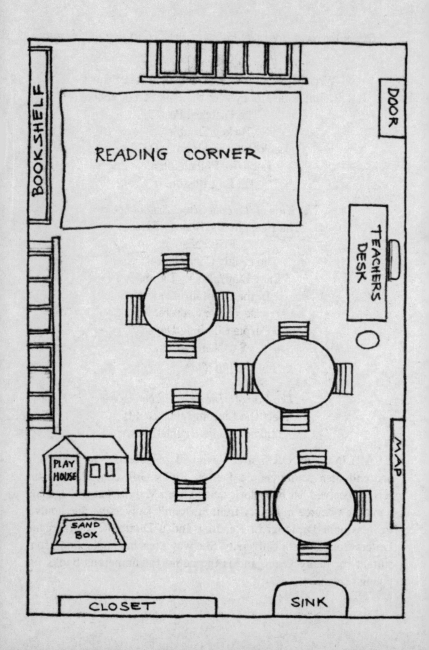

New Kids
4
at the Polk Street School

B-E-S-T Friends

Patricia Reilly Giff

Illustrated by Blanche Sims

A YOUNG YEARLING BOOK

Published by
Bantam Doubleday Dell Books for Young Readers
a division of
Bantam Doubleday Dell Publishing Group, Inc.
1540 Broadway
New York, New York 10036

ISBN: 0-440-40090-2

Printed in the United States of America

December 1988

31 30 29 28 27 26 25 24 23 22

CWO

For Irving and Betty Rockoff,
with love

CHAPTER
1

It was time for art.
Stacy Arrow looked at her paper.
She was going to draw a snowman.
A gorgeous one with a black hat.
She picked up her paintbrush.
A few drops of black landed on her shirt.
So what.
It was one of her father's old ones.
She painted the hat.

Then she dipped the brush into the white.

She made three fat lumps for the body.

She clicked her teeth.

Some of the black was mushing into the white.

"Can I borrow your clean brush?" she asked Eddie.

"Sure," he said. "I like the messy ones anyway."

She dipped Eddie's brush into the orange paint. She needed it for a carrot nose.

Perfect.

A black-and-white snowman.

Eddie leaned over. "Is that your cat?"

Stacy looked at her picture. "My cat?"

"That black thing." Eddie pointed. "Sitting in the snow."

"I guess so," Stacy said.

"What's his name?"

Stacy thought. She didn't even have a cat.

She crossed her fingers. "John."

Eddie started to laugh. "That's a boy's name."

"It's a boy cat."

Mrs. Zachary clapped her hands. "Time for snacks."

Snack bags were on the windowsill.

Stacy waited for Eddie to go first. She wanted to watch him hop.

Eddie was the best hopper in the class. He liked to hop all over the place.

They brought their bags back to the table.

Eddie opened his first.

He had a bunch of pretzels.

The salty kind.

Stacy's mouth watered.

She hoped she had something good too.

She opened her bag.

Yucks.

Bread and butter . . . with crusts.

Her father said crusts made your hair curl.

They didn't.

Stacy's hair was straight as a stick.

So was her sister Emily's.

Stacy tore the crust off the bread. She took a bite from the middle.

She was starving.

"Look, boys and girls," Mrs. Zachary said. She pointed.

Stacy looked up.

Outside a bird was sitting on the sill.

A brown-and-tan one.

"It's a sparrow," said Mrs. Zachary. She smiled at Stacy. "*Sparrow* sounds like *arrow*."

"My name," Stacy said.

"It's snowy outside," Jiwon said. "Maybe he's hungry."

Stacy pulled out her crusts. "He can have some of my snack."

"Are you sure?" Mrs. Zachary asked.

Stacy tried not to laugh. "I'm sure."

"Good girl," said Mrs. Zachary.

Slowly the teacher opened the window. A little snow blew inside.

The bird flew to the tree.

"Too bad," said A.J.

"Wait and see." Mrs. Zachary held up her hand. "Come on, Stacy."

Stacy went over to the window. She put her crusts on the ledge.

"Brrr," Mrs. Zachary said. "It's freezing out there."

She closed the window again.

A moment later the bird was back.

They watched him peck at the bread.

Another bird came.

Then a third.

Stacy kept watching. The first bird was watching her too. She was sure of it.

He loved crusts . . . just like her father.

"That bird gave me a great idea," said Mrs. Zachary. "Eat your snacks. Then come sit on the rug."

Stacy picked up her bread. She popped it into her mouth.

Everyone else was still eating.
Stacy looked at her snowman picture.
She laughed a little hum-hum laugh.
The snowman did look like a cat.
A black cat named John.
She stood up.
She went over to the rug.
She couldn't wait to hear Mrs. Zachary's
idea.

CHAPTER
2

It was dinnertime.

Stacy poked her head into the kitchen cabinet. She pulled out the plates.

It was her turn to set the table.

"Can't wait for tomorrow," she sang.

"Don't sing," said her sister, Emily.

"We're going for a walk," Stacy sang.

She put the spoons on the table. "A special walk."

She pulled out the forks.

She gave herself the best one. It had a flower on one end.

"We're going straight to Linden Avenue," she said. "To the pet store."

"I don't care," said Emily.

"That's not nice," their mother said.

"No, it isn't." Stacy gave Emily the bent fork.

A moment later their father came in.

"Some birds eat crusts," Stacy told him. "Some birds eat seeds."

He gave them a hug.

"Tomorrow we're going to buy some

seeds," she said. "It was Mrs. Zachary's idea."

"Time to eat," said their mother. She began to put out the food.

Emily frowned. "We have a spelling bee on Friday."

Stacy hopped to her chair.

She was trying to hop like Eddie . . . ten times without stopping.

"I hate spelling bees," Emily said. She picked up her fork. "I hate this fork too. All the points are wrong."

"I like my fork," Stacy said. She pushed a tomato off the edge of her plate. She stuck it underneath.

"I can't spell," said Emily.

"I can," Stacy said. *"Cat. C-a-t. Dog. D-o-g. No. N—"*

"Baby stuff." Emily looked as if she were going to cry.

"Don't worry," her mother said. "We'll help."

"Would," Emily said. *"W-o-u-l-d."*

"That's easy," said Stacy.

"Wouldn't," said Emily. "Which comes first? *D* or *n*?"

"N," said Stacy.

Her mother shook her head. "No. *D.*"

Emily made a face at Stacy. "Don't mix me up."

Stacy looked down at her plate.

Meat loaf in one spot.

String beans in another spot.

A lump of potatoes in another.

She gave her plate a spin.

The meat loaf ended up facing her.

Too bad.

She took a little bite. It tasted like cat food.

She spun the plate again. She was hoping for potatoes.

The string beans came up.

She took a long skinny one.

"Mother," said Emily. "Stacy's spinning her plate again."

Her mother looked up. "That's enough, Stacy."

"This isn't a circus," her father said. He winked at her.

"I just spun it a little." She stuck her tongue out at Emily. "You are *m-e-n*."

"What?"

"*Mean*, of course."

Emily laughed. "*M-e-e-n*."

"*M-e-a-n*," said their mother.

Stacy looked up.

No one was paying attention.

She gave her plate a tiny spin.

Good. Potatoes. The best thing.

She put some in her mouth.

Nice and soft.

She squished them back and forth in her mouth.

Emily saw her. "Horrible," she said.

"I wish you had some manners," said her mother.

Stacy looked down at her plate again. She was sick of manners. "I wish tomorrow was here," she said. "I wish it was walk time."

"Those walks aren't so hot," Emily said.

"How do you know?"

"I remember. It snowed on a walk we had. We couldn't even go."

"It's not going to snow," Stacy said.

"You're being *m-e-a-n* again," their mother told Emily.

"Yes," Stacy said.

"I'm sorry," Emily said. "I'm worried about spelling."

Stacy looked out the window. It was too dark to see.

Suppose it snowed tomorrow?

She crossed her fingers.

She looked down at her plate.

She'd give it a little spin.

Potatoes meant a sunny day.

Meat loaf meant snow.

She flicked the plate.

Meat loaf.

M-e-a-n, thought Stacy.

CHAPTER
3

It was a cold day.

The sun was shining though.

"Told you so-so-so," Stacy sang.

She sang it in a little voice.

She felt sorry for Emily.

Emily looked sad. She spelled all the way to school. *"Could. C-o-u-l-d."*

"Could go on a walk," Stacy sang to herself. "A wonderful walk."

"See you later," Emily said.

"See you too," said Stacy.

She marched down the hall. She went into her classroom.

It was early.

She was the first one there . . . except for Mrs. Zachary.

She looked out the window.

She wanted to see her bird.

A bunch of them were sitting on a roof.

They were too far to see.

Stacy said hello to Mrs. Zachary.

The teacher was drawing on the blackboard. First she drew a red bird. CARDINAL, she wrote underneath.

"That's a hard word," Stacy said.

Mrs. Zachary nodded. *"Car-di-nal."*

She drew a little brown bird. SPARROW, she wrote.

"Almost like my last name," Stacy said. *"Arrow."*

"Right." Mrs. Zachary smiled. "I'm glad you're here. I need a favor."

"Water the plants?"

Mrs. Zachary shook her head. "Better than that."

Stacy tried to think. She put her shoulders up in the air.

"We have a new girl." Mrs. Zachary drew a box. She wrote PET STORE. "She's coming today."

"That's nice."

"Annie," said Mrs. Zachary.

"Pretty good name," Stacy said.

"Would you be her partner?" Mrs. Zachary asked. "Walk with her?"

Stacy shook her head. "I can't. I'm walking with Jiwon."

"Jiwon could walk with Patty." Mrs. Zachary patted her shoulder. "Or Twana."

Stacy didn't say anything. She stuck out her lip.

"It's hard to get used to new things," said Mrs. Zachary. "Hard to get used to new people."

Stacy sat down at her table.

She watched Mrs. Zachary draw another bird. BLUE JAY.

"Poor Annie." Mrs. Zachary wiped her hands.

"All right." Stacy sighed. "I'll be her partner."

The door opened.

Eddie came in. So did A.J.

A few minutes later everyone was there.

Everyone but the new girl.

"I wore my brown boots," Jiwon said. "The strong ones. It's going to be cold outside."

Stacy swallowed. "I can't walk with you. I can't be your partner."

Jiwon brushed her hair back.

"I have to walk with the new girl," Stacy said. "Annie."

"You don't want to be my best friend?"

Stacy opened her mouth.

She wanted to say, "Yes, I do."

She wanted to tell Jiwon what Mrs. Zachary had said.

But then the door opened.

It was the new girl.

Her eyes were down.

So was her head.

Her hair stuck out all over.

"*Mess*," Stacy said in her head. "*M-e-s*."

She looked at Annie's jeans. A hole in one knee.

"Worse m-e-s," she sang.

"This is Annie," said Mrs. Zachary. "Our new friend."

Jiwon frowned at Stacy.

Mrs. Zachary pointed. "Sit next to Stacy."

Annie sat down.

She was making a noise. A whistling noise.

Stacy wished she could whistle too.

She tapped the new girl on the arm. "Don't whistle in the classroom."

The girl opened her mouth. Her two front teeth were missing.

She started to whistle again.

Eddie leaned over. "Tell that girl what to do."

Stacy looked at Annie.

"Unzip your jacket," she said. "Put your snack bag away."

She sighed.

Annie didn't do one thing right.

"Your jacket in the closet," Stacy said. "Your snack bag on the windowsill."

Annie was still whistling.

She was going to be a big pest. *P-a-s-t.*

CHAPTER
4

Everyone was running around.

A.J. watered the plants.

Jiwon put a sun on the calendar.

Mrs. Zachary called the roll. Then she looked around. "Everybody's here. Let's go."

The class put jackets on again.

Stacy wound her scarf around her neck. It was a little itchy.

So what. It was freezing outside.

She was going to need it.

The class lined up at the side of the room.

Annie was still sitting.

"Come on." Stacy pulled at her sleeve. "You're my partner."

Annie marched after her.

She was still whistling.

"We have to walk together," Stacy said.

Annie wiped her mouth with her hand. "Good." She grabbed Stacy's arm.

Stacy tried to pull away.

Annie held on tight.

Jiwon was walking with Twana.

She looked back over her shoulder.

She made a face at Stacy.

"Dumb kid." Annie sucked in her cheeks. "Tweet tweet," she whistled.

"That's my best friend," Stacy said.

Annie stopped whistling for a moment. "I'll be your best friend."

Stacy started to shake her head.

Then she saw Mrs. Zachary. She was watching them.

Stacy tried to smile. "We're going to the pet store."

"Going to buy a dog?"

"For the classroom? Don't be silly."

Jiwon looked back again.

Annie poked her chin out at Jiwon. She stuck her tongue where her teeth should be.

She looked horrible.

Stacy made an I'm-sorry face at Jiwon.

Jiwon didn't see. She had turned around again.

Stacy tried to pull her arm away from Annie.

But Annie held on tight. She stopped whistling. "Why are we going to the pet store?"

Stacy made believe she didn't hear her.

She didn't want to talk to that pain Annie. *P-a-n*.

Eddie and A.J. were marching behind them.

They were laughing.

Maybe they were laughing at Annie and her.

She didn't blame them.

They were zigzagging back and forth on the sidewalk.

Annie was trying to hold on to her arm.

Stacy tried to pull away.

"Why are we going to the pet store?" Annie shouted.

Mrs. Zachary looked back.

Stacy stopped pulling. "To buy birdseed," she said.

The class marched into the pet store.

A.J. and Eddie ran to look at the fish tank.

Blue and yellow fish were darting around like crazy.

Stacy stopped to look at the parrot.

He screeched in her ear.

Then they went to the back.

"We have a project," Mrs. Zachary told the man. "We're going to feed the birds this winter."

"We need seeds for the cardinals," Jiwon said.

"They love sunflower seeds," said the man. "You could have saved some from your garden."

"Too late now," said Mrs. Zachary. She looked out the door at the snow.

Everyone laughed.

"We need regular seed too," said Mrs. Zachary. "The juncos like that. So do the black-capped chickadees."

"Squirrels do too," said the man.

He picked out four big bags of seed.

Mrs. Zachary counted out the money.

Then they marched out the door again.

Annie grabbed Stacy's arm. "Wait for me."

They zigzagged up the street.

"Tweet, tweet," Annie whistled. "I'm a bird."

She laughed at her own joke.

Her own horrible joke, Stacy thought.

Stacy wondered how to spell *horrible*.

Annie was horrible.

Her face was horrible.

So was her whistling.

Stacy sighed.

She had a horrible new best friend.

H-a-r-a-b-l.

CHAPTER
5

It was Wednesday. Stacy took another magazine from the pile.

She was cutting out good breakfast pictures.

So was the rest of the class.

Next to her Annie was cutting out a potato.

It was a fat brown one.

She was whistling too.

Stacy tapped her on the arm. "Wrong," she said. "All wrong."

Annie stopped whistling. She rubbed her hands on her jeans. "I don't care. I like potatoes."

Stacy started to laugh.

She thought about cutting out potato chips.

Mrs. Zachary would have a fit.

So would her mother.

She had to eat cereal, or eggs and toast.

She began to cut out an orange. It was hard to make the scissors go right.

The orange kept getting smaller.

Eddie leaned over. "Look at that dumb

Annie," he said. "She's cutting out a terrible breakfast."

Stacy laughed. She looked out the window. "When are we going to give out bird food?" she asked Mrs. Zachary.

Mrs. Zachary shook her head. "You forgot something."

Stacy sighed. She raised her hand.

"Good girl," said Mrs. Zachary. "We'll go outside soon. Do your breakfast pictures first."

"I can't think." Jiwon put her hands over her ears.

"Me neither," said Patty. "It's all that whistling."

Annie stopped whistling. She started to sing. "Doodle doodle do. Doodle d—"

Mrs. Zachary clapped her hands. "We don't like to disturb people."

Annie stopped singing in the middle of a doodle.

Her mouth stayed open.

Stacy tried not to laugh. Sometimes Annie was a funny girl.

Too bad she was spoiling everything.

Too bad she was making Jiwon mad at her.

Stacy turned to a new page.

Her orange was no good.

No good at all.

It looked like a Life Saver.

A skinny little Life Saver.

Stacy kept turning the pages.

Nothing for breakfast.

Soup. Carrots. Milk.

Great. Milk. She could use that.

She began to cut.

Next to her Annie was cutting too.

She was cutting a cup of tea.

"Kids don't drink tea," Stacy told her.

Annie put her lips together.

She whistled a little whistle.

"This is my grandfather's breakfast," she said. "Tomatoes, potatoes, and tea."

"I never heard of a breakfast like that."

"I know," said Annie. "That's what he eats though."

Stacy raised her shoulders in the air.

"I'm going to give this paper to him. It's his birthday. He'll love it."

Stacy nodded. "Nice."

"Everyone finished?" Mrs. Zachary asked.

Stacy looked at her paper.

She had a wiggly glass of milk.

A skinny little orange.

A piece of toast.

Not such a great breakfast.

"Who would like to show his breakfast?" Mrs. Zachary asked.

Jiwon raised her hand. She went to the front.

"This is my breakfast," she said. "Juice, milk, Sugar Pops."

Mrs. Zachary nodded.

Eddie was next.

He had a huge breakfast.

Grapefruit. Toast. Pancakes. Bacon. Milk.

Eddie loved to eat.

"How about you, Annie?" the teacher asked.

Annie went to the front.

She held up her pictures.

Everyone looked at the fat potato, the red tomato, the tea.

They started to laugh.

Mrs. Zachary frowned at the class. "That's a different breakfast," she told Annie. "An interesting one."

Stacy waited for Annie to tell about her grandfather.

Annie didn't though.

She just sat down.

Her face was red.

Stacy went up next.

She showed her breakfast.

"I love oranges," Jiwon said.

Stacy smiled at Jiwon.

Jiwon smiled back.

They were friends again.

Then she looked at Annie.
Annie's head was down.
Maybe Annie wished she were home.
Home with her grandfather.

CHAPTER
6

Today was snowy.

"I have a surprise," Mrs. Zachary said. "Bundle up. We'll go outside."

Everyone ran for jackets.

Stacy sat on the floor. She had to put on her boots.

They were her old ones. Her good ones were wet.

It was a hard job.

She was hot. Her face felt red.

Annie sat on the floor too.

She pushed on Stacy's boots.

Stacy pulled.

"No good," said Annie.

"These are my old boots."

Annie sat back. "How did you get them on before?"

Stacy raised her shoulders. "My mother."

Annie leaned forward again. "Take off your sneakers. Wear your boots over your socks."

Stacy thought for a moment. Then she laughed.

She tugged off her sneakers. She threw them in the closet.

Then she slipped on her boots.

They went down the hall.

"Tweet, tweet," Annie whistled.

Stacy drew her lips together. She tried to whistle too.

Maybe Mrs. Zachary was right, she thought. You had to get used to new people, new things.

The nurse poked her head out her door. "Not so noisy," she said.

Stacy and Annie looked at each other.

They closed their mouths.

They rushed outside.

Everyone was running around.

Stacy ran around too.

Her boots kept slipping.

Her feet were cold. They felt terrible.

"Here comes the surprise," Mrs. Zachary said.

She clapped her hands.

Her clapping sounded different. That was because she was wearing gloves.

Jim came outside. He was the man who cleaned up.

In his hand was a long pole. In the other was a little stand.

He smiled at them. "Is this the bird-feeding class?"

Everyone laughed.

They marched around to the side of the building. "We're going to put this feeder here," said Jim.

"Right in front of our classroom," said Mrs. Zachary.

"We'll be able to watch the birds," said Jiwon. She smiled at Stacy.

Jim took a hammer out of his overalls pocket. He put the pole into the ground.

He hammered the stand on top.

Stacy was freezing.

She stamped her feet.

She was sorry she had taken off her sneakers.

Mrs. Zachary poured seed on the stand. "Now we have to wait."

Stacy put her hands in her pockets.

The birds were on the roof of a house next door.

She wished they'd hurry. She couldn't wait to get inside.

Then a bird came. Another one came too.

"Look," said Mrs. Zachary. "There's a purple finch."

"He doesn't look purple to me," A.J. said.

"No," said Mrs. Zachary. "He has a rosy color."

"He looks like a raspberry," Annie said.

Everyone laughed.

"I'll call more of them," Annie said. She began to whistle.

The birds on the stand flew away.

They didn't come back.

"Don't worry," Mrs. Zachary said. "They will."

The class marched inside.

Annie was last.

"Annie spoiled everything," someone said.

"Annie and her whistling," said someone else.

Stacy looked to see where Mrs. Zachary was.

She was at the front. She hadn't heard.

"Annie had a silly breakfast," someone said.

Stacy took a breath. "And you made my feet cold."

Annie looked at the ground.

She looked as if she wanted to cry.

Stacy stamped up the stairs.

She felt *m-e-a-n.*

CHAPTER

7

Stacy was having a bad dream.

It was about Annie . . . and a stomach ache.

She opened her eyes.

It was a real stomach ache.

She pulled the blanket over her head. "Call Mommy," she told Emily. "I'm *s-i-k*."

"*S-i-c-k*," said Emily. "Even I know that."

Stacy was glad she was sick.

She wouldn't have to go to school.

She wouldn't have to see Annie.

She wouldn't have to see anybody.

Her mother came into the bedroom. "Too bad. No school, I guess."

"I guess not," Stacy said.

She closed her eyes.

She could hear Emily getting dressed.

Emily went downstairs.

It was quiet in the bedroom. Very quiet.

After a while Stacy pulled the blanket off her head.

"Good-bye," she heard Emily tell their mother.

Stacy went to the window.

She wanted to wave to Emily.

Emily didn't see her.

Stacy banged on the window.

Emily didn't hear her.

Emily wasn't worried about her sister.
Her poor sick sister.

Stacy went back to bed.

She was getting hungry.

She thought of a potato.

That would be good.

Delicious.

That made her think of Annie.

She didn't want to think about Annie
though.

She wished she hadn't said that about her feet being cold.

She wished she had said potatoes were a good breakfast.

Especially for a grandfather.

Stacy could feel her stomach begin to ache.

Her mother came into the room. "Maybe you could eat a little breakfast."

"Maybe," said Stacy.

She put on her bathrobe.

She put on Emily's fuzzy slippers.

She went downstairs with her mother.

"Do you want cornflakes?" her mother asked.

Stacy shook her head.

"Toast?"

"No," Stacy said. "Tea and potatoes, please. No tomato."

Her mother smiled. "It will take a little while."

She put a potato in the microwave oven.

Stacy sat there waiting.

Her mother sat down next to her. "Sometimes you can get a stomach ache when you worry."

"Not me," said Stacy.

"No," said her mother. "Sometimes you can get one when you're afraid."

"Not me," Stacy said again.

Her mother looked up at the ceiling. "How about when you're sorry for something?"

Stacy looked at the tea kettle.

She kept blinking.

She didn't want to cry.

Her mother didn't say anything. She got up to pour the tea.

A little tea.

A lot of milk.

"This will make you feel better," said her mother.

"I know." Stacy took a sip.

"It's always good to say you're sorry," her mother said.

"That's what I do," said Stacy.

"Yes," said her mother.

"That's what I'm going to do."

"Good idea."

They didn't say anything for a while.

"What about other kids?" Stacy asked. "Kids who should be sorry."

Her mother sighed.

She got up to see if the potato was ready. "You do the right thing, Stacy. Show everybody else."

"That's hard."

Her mother nodded.

"Suppose they don't pay attention?"

Her mother took out the potato. "Hot!" She looked at Stacy. "Keep trying."

Stacy watched her mother cut the potato. She put butter on top.

Her mother smiled. "Potatoes are good for breakfast."

"My stomach ache is better," Stacy said. "I'm going to school."

Her mother shook her head. "Too late. I don't have the car today."

"I'm going to miss stuff," Stacy said. "We're going to cut out good lunches."

"Sorry," her mother said.

Stacy stamped up to her room.

She didn't have anything to do.

She hated this whole day.

CHAPTER
8

"Today is my spelling bee," Emily said.

Stacy hopped into the schoolyard behind her.

"Good hopping," Emily said.

"Getting good," said Stacy.

"Today is the worst day." Emily looked sad. *"W-o-r-s-t."*

"Poor Emily." Stacy took a huge hop.

"Today is a good day for me. I'm going to feed my *s-p-a-r-r-o-w*, sparrow."

Emily looked surprised. "How did you know that?"

Stacy laughed. "It's just like our name."

Stacy waved to Emily. She hopped down the hall.

Her classroom door was open.

Almost everyone was there.

Stacy hung up her jacket.

Then the class stood. They were going to say the Pledge.

They had just learned it.

Stacy made believe she knew all the words.

She didn't though.

She kept getting mixed up.

She'd have to get used to it.

Just like hopping.

Everyone sat down.

"Who has something for show-and-tell?" Mrs. Zachary asked.

Stacy went first.

"That's only fair," said Mrs. Zachary. "Poor Stacy missed school yesterday."

Stacy took a breath. "I have a lot to tell."

"I bet it's about being sick," said Eddie.

"Yes. It was lonesome. I missed everybody."

"We missed you too," Mrs. Zachary said.

"I missed Jiwon, and Twana, and A.J., and Patty, and Eddie."

She looked at Annie. "I missed Annie too. I like to hear her whistle."

Annie put her lips together. "Tweet tweet."

"Annie has lots of ideas," Stacy said. "About boots . . .

"That wasn't such a good idea," Annie said.

"About potatoes." Stacy took a little hop. "Potatoes are nice and soft. They're good when you're sick. That's what I had for breakfast."

"Really?" Jiwon asked.

"Just like Annie said."

Annie nodded. "Just like my grandfather said."

Stacy sat down.

Mrs. Zachary smiled. "You know what I love to see?"

She looked around. "I love to see that all of you are friends."

"Me too," said Eddie.

"Me too," said Jiwon.

"Tweet," said Annie.

"Hey." Stacy stood up again. "I forgot something."

She went to the front. She held up a

brown bag. "I brought a bunch of stuff for the birds."

Everyone looked at the bag.

"Crusts," said Stacy. "A piece of apple."

"Good idea," said Mrs. Zachary.

"And a piece of bacon."

Everyone laughed.

"My mother said birds like that."

As soon as show-and-tell was over, they put jackets on.

They rushed outside.

Stacy's mother was right.

The birds loved the bacon.

They all came down to eat.

Then the doors opened.

Stacy turned around.

It was Emily's class.

Emily had a star pasted on her forehead. "I won the spelling bee," she told everyone. "I spelled the hardest word."

Stacy smiled at Emily. "What was it?"

"*Sparrow*," said Emily. "The word was *sparrow*."

They looked at each other. They started to laugh.

Stacy took a couple of hops. She hugged Emily.

Jiwon started to hop too.

Then Twana.

"Come on, Annie," they yelled.
"Tweet," Annie whistled.
Stacy put her lips together.
She was going to learn to whistle next.

Travel Fun with the Polk Street Kids on Tour

Join them as they take to the road to see America. Each fun-filled story includes a kid's guide to the city featuring the best attractions, museums, monuments, maps, and more!

10 A Polk Street Special

Oh Boy, Boston!
The Polk Street Kids on Tour

Includes the Polk Street Guide to Visiting Boston

0-440-41365-6

6 A Polk Street Special

A YEARLING BOOK

Look Out, Washington, D.C.!
Patricia Reilly Giff

Includes the Polk Street Guide to Visiting Washington, D.C.

Illustrated by Blanche Sims

0-440-40934-0

9 A Polk Street Special

Next Stop, New York City!
The Polk Street Kids on Tour
Patricia Reilly Giff

Includes The Polk Street Guide to Visiting New York City

Illustrated by Blanche Sims

0-440-41362-1

Available from Yearling Books

JFic
E
Gif

Giff, Patricia
Reilly.

B-E-S-T friends.

DATE			